Postcard
from Idaho

By Aleka
 Waters and
 Sibylle Bonheur

This book is dedicated to the memory of Lady Neptune.

"Some people hear voices that are in them with a rare clarity, and they obey what they hear. They then become either crazy or they become legends.

Jim Harrison Legends of the Fall

There are only fragments of you and fragments of my soul and it's in bits that I will write your story or mine or can be ours because everything today mixes and becomes confused as mists of a memory in which I swim like your vacillations on this highway on which you're falling down. This fog paralyzes me in one way, but in another I am pleased ...

There will be no structure to this story, it will come uncertain and wandering, as my mind that swims in the land of remembrance. It flies, volatile from the clouds as the last ode that my soul sang, like the swan song, incomplete and inconsistent. It will be the unpredictable flow of the river that takes our lives in these other dimensions where everything is eternal.

I begin at the end or the middle part of a dream where the ghosts of the past come to whisper the sweet melody of what exists only in our memories...
I too seek the way to my home and

my past, as do you.

I cling to this postcard you sent me from beyond ... This is the remains of another world, or the letter came from another reality and this road that never ends becomes an infinite river where phosphorescent waves of our souls, dance and abandon themselves to their fate without being able to fight.

I also became the river, the pool where I strolled, eventually in a hypnotic state, I am lured into another world. Did I drown or perhaps did I only refresh? One way or another, I always travel in its clear waters ...
I only remember the blue bird, the bird of paradise fluttering above its deep waters. He invited me out there and I surely wanted to join him, indifferent to the risk I was taking because I know there is no border between life and death, dream and reality. The Bluebird invited me to

jump into the clouds
hovering above the mysterious wave.
Languid and ethereal, tired of my
solitude and sadness, I listened to
what his silent voice whispered in my
ear.
"Jump in these clouds and let them
wash you from your past lives.
immerse in the wave and you'll be
reborn, infinite ..."

I cannot remember the rest, only this
adventure with this blonde boy who
appeared to me under a waterfall in
the middle of the dance of the mists.
We lived like bohemians and today
his poetry still fills my soul. He was
a poet a beautiful soul and he knew in
this journey between two worlds I
would dance over his musings. He
waited for me for a long time in that
other kingdom and knew my face
well before he met me.

There are these moments of
eternity that haunt me and
make faint

the hands of time. Despite the years, which can often erase the memories, they can never reduce the imprint that love leaves forever in our hearts. A few seconds is all it takes, a fleeting spark that sets fire to the whirlwind of our memories and it is in the transience of this flash that we feel most alive. This is where our divinity is revealed and where the heart stores and feels the merger with complete unity.

There is no more time, there is no more space, there is no more than the language of the soul and this invitation to travel in places that only insiders can enter. Everything changes in the tsunami of emotions, reborn from the deepest despair. It is these unexpected moments that leave the infinite feeling of magic around us. It is for this quivering of our souls, these moments of eternity which thunder, that make our existence worthwhile. Time is like a river you cannot touch the same water twice since the current is ongoing, but the source that fills your heart is eternal.

This boy that I met in the waters of the river is in my mind, the guardian of another world. He is a poet, a philosopher who taught spirituality and magic in our meetings. He is the prince of my nebula. Perhaps it is the spirit of the river, he is of no earthly kingdom, but for me he remains the gypsy that I met on the roads of Idaho. You will certainly not come across it or him in the territory of Idaho because it is an invented Idaho, an Idaho that has only ever existed in my heart. One day, I will leave the banks of this river, I let myself drift like a giant lotus on the river that takes travelers to the land of Idaho.

The blue bird of paradise flew again and again over that mysterious utopia born from the meanderings of my fertile psyche and transports newcomers to the realm of childhood and endless parties.

No bad queen reigns over this dream world, who's borders are as changeable as the clouds. I look forward to seeing the giant sequoia, which stands in the meadow dotted with sunflowers, because on top of that tree is where the lost paradise of my youth is to be found. Only the chosen few know the secret code to enter the cabin on top of trees. The Idaho traveler then accesses this magical place where you can forever relive the memories of innocence on earth forever lost, but these fleeting visions disappear at the first morning dew.

The Prince of Idaho is this fair young man asleep on the road, cool as ice, who dreams of the faded childhood he will never find on this earth. He dreams of his home, although he will never return to this earth. On this road that never ends, the Prince of Idaho joined the clouds where he takes me with him whenever

life becomes too painful. So, when I feel this angst well
up in me I fall asleep and find the Prince of Idaho and my lost utopia.
In this magical land, your only treasure is your heart and the dancing salmon making their way in earnest up the rivers.
We are all sunflower loving gypsies who merrily embrace on coffins at funerals.
We're dressed in pink
bathrobes and steal
motorcycles.
The corruption of society by money has long since passed out of this world beyond time and space.
The Prince of Idaho flies away, as if a cloud of smoke. He occasionally sends me postcards of this country that exists only in the chimeras to tell me that on this road that does not end, there's love and hope.

"As the Prince of Idaho, I am

sending you postcards to

tell you our story and I always come back to this endless road on which I had to say goodbye to my past, but I also go back to the river when the asphalt becomes water." Oh river, your deep waters penetrate my soul and bring me into the deep dimensions of my being. The plasticity of your waves create in me the original memory of the rich waters of our birth. As the fetus in the womb, we always come back in your womb to immerse ourselves in this out of time memory and this deep and mysterious silence of your incessant murmur, as if to hear the echo back to the forgotten dimensional surface.

You're the water from the source of life, you are the water of the river that came to me to blend and mix my tears. In your melting pot, all the faces of humanity mingle and mix and eventually purify the beauty of one. Within your waters prevail gods and guardians of the cosmic memory, matching the movement and fertility of universal harmony.

Oh river, your waters become waterfalls that flow deep in my inner worlds and your purity and silence wash and cleanse my mortal sins.

Spirit of the River, Prince of Idaho, some say you're only an imaginary friend, but it seemed you were real when you came to talk to me in the depths of despair. You are my most intimate and closest friend, the one who will never abandon me and will always haunt my memories. In the kingdom of souls, I have the feeling that you expect and that you watch over me on this long lonely and difficult road of life. Whenever I think of you, you seem to instil in me nostalgia of this lost paradise.

But my true story, that of Laura River, is not limited to a dream between two worlds or to the tale of this poetic meeting. I come back to the roots of my life, these currents both intrepid and whirlpools that have shaped my soul and bring out the spirit of the shaman of my being.

No one knows when the great spirit will remind me to him, or when he 'll come to light my divine spark to make it to the stars. I was born when leaves crackle and when they are adorned in orange and yellow colors of autumn, my master is Scorpio; the Plutonian influences make sense in me, due to the attraction to the mystery and hidden things. I was born November 3, 1983 at 20:30; My ascendant is the sign of cancer and it is no wonder that nostalgia of childhood and the world of dreams haunts my heart. These two water signs, signs of the unconscious and of mediumship predispose me to some gifts that will fully

Awaken in me later in my life. I lived a happy childhood until I was ten years old in 1993. That year will mark the end of my carelessness and break my heart deeply. Unknowingly, this will correspond, without my knowing at the time to the death of my soul mate. It appears that at the dawn of my life, my destiny was already cursed by the loss of which I was then unaware. His existence as mine, seem to mark the seal of a dark curse.

I go through life events that are eerily similar of those experienced by the Prince of Idaho in his lifetime. I'm in this old, too conventional Europe, persecuted by my classmates, rejected for years and suffering constant humiliation.
I develop the strange feeling of speaking a language unknown to most people.
My heart is still pure as the child

away from the corruptions of the

youth of the time. This rejection and marginality mirror's the story of my soulmate, despite different contexts.

On another continent, many years ago, the Prince of Idaho suffers the same problems as me, but much earlier in his life.
Child of hippies in the 70's, he will live like a heavenly tramp, a missionary of God, on the road, traveling from city to city until South America. He knows not only material poverty, but also rejection and isolation that I myself have suffered. Maybe our souls are too wild to be tamed, maybe the sacred fire consumes us in flames and such too wild, drunk on freedom, the society cannot close its walls in on us.

Since the death of my soulmate, I went in search of a truth that only my prince of Idaho knew since his childhood, that of a force greater than the origin of anything.

My only friend as a mother, a sister is my faithful dog Lady Neptune and will remain until my 29th year, when it will join the stars. From my childhood I am defending the oppressed and the humiliated and I feel close to the societally excluded. Just like my soulmate, I have the desire to avoid pain to any living creature, I therefore become vegetarian. Two major events will change my destiny, my first love and my initiatory journey in America will affect me deeply. It is a real thunderbolt which embodies my ideal of the great romantic and charming prince of love in my heart, that of an innocent maiden. My spirituality and my ability to mediumship have not yet awakened, but I already feel very attracted by the Amerindian universe; this is not simply a superficial appeal to their folklore and customs, but a stronger connection that I can even understand. The Prince of Idaho had the same fascination with Native Americans and the same psychic abilities as me and he will discover later in his life, like me, that Indian blood flowed in his veins during one of his previous lives; the Hopi Indians. During my stay on Indian lands of Monument Valley, Arizona, sand that I rubbed on the palms of my hands and my face penetrate me with a primal energy, a wild drive which I can't yet understand the origin and the infinite desert seems to speak a mysterious language to my heart; one of the authentic purity of the origins of life.

I also have a youthful passion for the orca; I am fascinated by the power and majesty of the mighty predator I had occasion at my thirteen years to approach and this is subconsciously I get in touch with my totem animal that sends me his power that I connect with. which is called the wolf of the sea. I kiss his rough skin and look deep into his eyes and I read the depth of his core.

I contemplate the look of the noble killer whale which appears to me as if dice often in dreams during my younger years, sending me his bravery and courage to endure the difficult trials of my existence.

The black part of the orca's coat hides it under the surface while swimming between two waters and the white part of its coat helps conceal the prey he covets in the depths of the ocean.

The orca appears to me as a magnetic and proud warrior, clever and mysterious that knows how to stay in the shade and pop up when you least expect it. I recognize myself in the instinct of the animal apparently peaceful and very sharpened in its perceptions. Orca groups visit my dreams in my sleep and dance spirals around galaxies drawing the Eight of infinity in a universal harmony as if to remember the immemorial memory of the Nation of Heaven.

Orcas are the guardians of cosmic memory in shamanism, which fully takes its meaning in my life many years later and after a long spiritual journey.

Going back to that first love, the first event that will change my life and take me on strange paths. It is not only my first love I encounter it is through the eyes of this boy that the original memory of the universe visits me. Indeed, from the eyes of this young man Gaspard, emanates an immaterial and impalpable energy. This is not an animal of fluid physics that we know in our reality. This fluid, I understand much later, is the memory of the connection between souls.

This sensation will upset me and the love that never materializes due to sad circumstances would break me but put me on the track of the divine source experimentally.

Without ever realizing this romance because of shyness and lack of understanding of both young people and the departure of the teen without trace, not only will that first love plunge my life into chasms of pain, but it also will allow me to recover the reminiscence of a first memory that actually predates the universe. The end of high school persecutions and the loss of that love leave me profoundly misguided. Yet literary at heart, I chose to study law as if to lose a little more and confront myself with the brutality of a conformist society that I reject. I feel like a caged animal in this law school where the lives of future lawyers already seem mapped out. I myself, intensely suffer in silence, unable to find my place among the other students, putting myself away. I feel a deep rage against society, against the world against this golden youth which does not question the established values. I feel a great inner turmoil that I cannot identify and which I cannot name the cause, I understand in hindsight I felt the wrath of the warrior shaman. I was feeling more-or-less buried deep within myself, but I know now that we can't give up what one is and ignore the call of the soul. My heart still heavily borrowed from the world of childhood struggles to channel the conflicting impulses that inhabit it.

Still haunted by the first injury I met, by chance, a gypsy woman in the street near my university has a special aura. The depth of her eyes and the glow that emanates leave me in no doubt that she has a special gift. With a simple touch of the hand, she evokes the loss of first love, she gives me several specific pieces of information relative to this boy and our futures together, I mention this notion of fluid that I felt with that boy and the gypsy predicted to me the qualities of mediumship that will thrive. Hypersensitive fragile and vulnerable, I do not really believe in the development of these capacities and am not ready yet. The gypsy predicts in minute detail the return of the young man a day in my life. I sense the sincerity in that look, and I trust her. That prediction held me for twelve years.

The Prince of Idaho, at that time is already dead for many years and I still do not know our link, but he knew before his death that our destinies were linked. He had indeed seen a vision of his future wife and had made a portrait of her. He had to meet in 2002 year of the prediction of the gypsy, but how to make me understand that I was not yet awake, the link between soul mates, between him who was dead and myself, I just was not ready to take notice. Reassured by predicting the return of my first love, I see myself slightly reassured. I am weak, but primal forces are in me and an inner rage, aggression that is not unlike that of the bear. I've always worn around my neck this Indian necklace with a bear paw pendant I brought back from Arizona and the Navajo crafts. This youth trip to the United States has changed my life and that which the shaman unconsciously awakened within me. I start getting interested in spiritism of Allan Kardec and the survival of the soul, but still not arriving to understand fully the nature of the afterlife.

To free me from my anguish and my shyness and to numb my pain for not finding my place in this world, I gradually steal benzodiazepines prescribed to my Mother by her doctor. These abuses eventually lead me to a terrible experience. Having a strong dose of drugs mixed with vodka, I get mugged one night by a brute and soulless man, abusing my unconsciousness to achieve his ends. I feel broken and dirty because I wanted to offer my virginity to my first love. After this traumatic experience, I decide to end a life without the slightest glimmer of hope. The night before, I try an experience of spiritualism as a kind of ultimate cry for help, what I don't know is that spiritualism attracts negative entities and my first session was at 21 years of age, I also had my first vision of the face of my grandfather in a flash of white light lasting for a few seconds. His face was rejuvenated and bright. He whispered to me "you know I love you!" but as for my first vision, I did not have the certainty of his grainy reality despite my heart always recognized it as genuine.

Two years later, my 23rd year, the age at which the Prince of Idaho died, I see my grandfather after the attack, towards dawn, where pills in my nightstand wait to be ingested, I am suddenly aware of my state of sleep, at least, that of my body, as if I was awake. I can see the room around me, and my lit lamp, I'm lying sideways when suddenly I feel a presence behind me; very surprised by this strange feeling, I mentally asked "who's there?" With amazement I hear the natural response of my grandfather who tells me telepathically that it is him. I wait a few seconds before responding to him, that's when my spiritual body turns back, but not my body of flesh.

I feel my etheric body move in my physical body. What lightness, what fluidity, what obvious sensation of feeling my soul moving in the grace of its subtle body, as if I were reliving an experience of a distant memory that had been buried deep within.

To see my grandfather, appear to me as he was when I knew him when I was a little girl and share a few words with him fascinates me at the highest level. I contemplate him for a second; he confirms that it is him that I have seen in my first vision and delivers me these few words, "you will soon meet your husband." This vision of my grandfather and the feeling of my own soul, on one hand saves me from death and on the other, leads me on mysterious paths. I develop the gift of writing and I undertake the journey of perception as many others had done so before me. I am aware of all the mysteries of life and the universe around us and I try to understand the invisible realities that lurk in the shadows and in our unconscious as the secret of our origins in the infinite cosmos.

I first expressed my feelings through a shamanic and mystical prose that seems to flow naturally from my soul, like automatic writing.

Religion did not call to me and I had not been raised in this world, but I feel that my mind has always felt the shiver of another reality and what may lie beyond. I wanted to understand the nature of these subtle energies that drive us, and I have seen the reality of the divine by powerful mystical experiences.

I decided to return to the plains of Arizona on the trail of a powerful shaman who will guide me in this initiation. I met Aleka at a Navajo reservation near Monument Valley, this meeting will be the scent of a dream. We only stay three days together, but in this time my soul remembers a previous life and the reality of eternity. Aleka, following the traditional rituals makes me swallow hallucinogenic mushrooms 3 times to access the world of vision.

I will forever be changed by these trips in parallel worlds. In a trance that will last only a few seconds but in which I lose control of myself, comes the memory of an oh so painful and dizzying previous life. I always felt I was carrying the memory of humiliation and guilt and a sacrificial death and subsequently, even though I was born female, it was no surprise to learn that I was a man in a former life.

Then this voice emerges from my heart and delivers a secret from the depths of my being and of the universe: "I am Tassem" If this revelation seems very strange at first, it delivers me from a great inner pain and my eyes shine a bright light.

The divine spark seems to live again in me and fills me with a deep sense of joy. Aleka says to me that I am a prophetess and that my experiences are not the result of chance. He explains that Tassem, known as the guardian of the memory of the soul among Amerindians, well away from the myth that we have built around him, is primarily a shaman who understood the laws of the energy that govern the universe. He explains that I came back to clear this message choked by legends and predicted that I'll give the word of the universal source in a book: the phoenix of our souls. I questioned the choice of this title and he said that one day I will meet another of my spirit totem animals: the phoenix.

Aleka gives me one last dose of sacred mushrooms, at this moment I reach enlightenment, the experience described by many mystics; literally divine light fills my soul and my whole being, I am the light and I merge with it in a radiation, feeling eternal. I am the One and all at once in this light and in this state of deep bliss and harmony that fills my being for several hours, I feel the merger and the interconnection with all that lives on the Earth and in the universe. I belong to the enlightened people who understand the law of the universe. I know this link with the light is unwavering and forever illuminates my soul. My mystical theory of the word of the source, the phoenix of our souls gradually takes shape. The doors of perception have opened for me. William Blake, Huxley, Kerouac and dear Mojo Risin have been there. The great Jim Morrison dictates poems to me through shamanic trance, I feel fulfilled and finally on the way to happiness.

But did I forget the vision that I had of my life under the influence of sacred mushrooms? This painting began moving, darkening shadows, a girl, her head down and barely concealing her stricken face. A figure came alive and took the appearance of my mother who will always be in my life my most faithful support, with the guardian of my soul, my faithful Lady Neptune, but despite the shadows, light still shone after it passed by, but did I forget this seance of spiritism when the word treason had appeared? Yet I have faith in the future and in my grandfather, who predicted to me that I would soon meet my husband and for me it could only be my first love.

The dream breaks when I discover September 22nd, 2011 that this boy is married for a couple of years; in my purity and my innocence, I thought he would come back into my life as the gypsy had foretold to me. I am alone in my grief with

Lady Neptune, my little dog who falls ill. That's when I'm about to die by excess of alcohol, then in an altered state of consciousness, I see my second animal totem arise out of my chest. This is a large and majestic phoenix with glowing wings and there comes to me a distant melody that appears to me suddenly familiar.

It seems to me to be the theme of the movie, Brazil. This sound comes from a male voice I did not know at first, without ever having paid attention before, I seem to recognize that tone of voice, but it's as though I'm hearing it for for the first time...It is the voice of the Prince of Idaho. This cursed artist died many years ago, but his song keeps coming into my memory and his words captivate me and comfort me, its vulnerability and sensitivity touch me deeply. It seems I recognize and perceive the cracks of his soul as a reflection of my own cracks, it seems to me I recognize the Prince of Idaho, literally. I travel along the path left by the Prince of Idaho and feel suddenly drawn into a strangely familiar universe. Many similarities between his personal story and mine are emerging. The rejection suffered in his youth, physical abuse that he suffered as his escape into drugs and alcohol to forget, bring me to my own journey. Shaman powers and medium abilities of the prince of Idaho fascinate me very much.

He also had access to mystical revelations under the influence of sacred plants and was one of the awake people. The number 3, one of the Holy Trinity, kept appearing in his dates of birth and death. His astral configuration was strangely close to mine, especially that he also was born under the constellation of the Phoenix. The Prince of Idaho comforts my broken heart. Lady Neptune is sick and my book for now does not work out. Everything collapses around me, since the breakdown of this prediction about my first love, if the phoenix appears at this point in my life, where everything has become brutally broken, would it be the promise of one day to be reborn? But where? In this life or elsewhere? Comes the moment the Prince of Idaho finally appears to me, four months after the strange chance which had brought him my way. Drowned in drugs and alcohol, I feel like I'm close to death, the Prince of Idaho seems to be the only person to hold on to. I knew a soul was nearby but had never considered his coming. It was then that I see him for the first time.

The Prince of Idaho stands beside me in the dark, I see his emergence in the shadows, the perfection of his regular features. His long blonde hair gives to him an angelic aura. He's cold and full of cracks and blue eyes that had so challenged me, seem full of mystery.

I raise with him the memory of his painful first love and ask if his true soulmate had done this first birth injury that was imprinted on his heart. He remains silent, but when I ask him:

"And me, would you have loved me?" He turns to face me and from that look of ice, at first cold and full of wounds, popped the warmth of unconditional love that troubles me deeply.

I awake with a start at dawn, first thinking of a dream despite the sense of reality that emanates from this first vision.

While I wonder about the reality of this apparition, when I return to my room, in the doorway I hear a popping noise coming from the room, this is where I see a postcard. which was stuck on top of a shelf, literally be moved in the air about five meters and be placed at the foot of my bed at the other end of the room.

On this Christmas card that my mother had given to me, it says "Laura, you're a girl full of surprises in this great adventure of life. I wish that all your dreams come true. I love you, mom." I have never witnessed such a phenomenon, but on the other hand I do not wonder, it seems natural to me. This reminds me of an episode in the life of the Prince of Idaho when lost and alone in the abyss of existence, he only had a postcard sent long ago by his mother to hold on to. I feel that this postcard is a positive sign from the Prince of Idaho from Heaven and a promise of something brilliant in my life.

A few days later, the Prince of Idaho reappears in a vision. This time, the doubt is no longer possible. It seems that I have medium abilities that the gypsy had repeatedly detected in me which are now confirmed. I am sleeping, or rather my physical body is asleep when I feel at some point that something tickles my hand, then I feel my soul awaken and with the eyes of my soul I can see my physical self sleeping.

I feel a presence in my

back, thus the Prince of Idaho manifests his arrival.

As always, I'm never really prepared to live this kind of experience with the other world and express telepathically in reply, "I'm afraid to see you."

There is at that time a kind of astral projection, I then find myself face to face with the prince's etheric body. He has blonde hair and a half long, bright red sweater, thick wool knit with a raised twisted and embossed pattern, high quality pants in black made of cotton and polyester giving him a beautiful fall with a beautiful cut green tweed jacket at his first coming. Seeing him in such detail fascinates me to no end; I am overwhelmed by his presence.

This meeting appears stunning and natural. Amazed by this vision, I tell him telepathically, "You're an angel, you're a child of the stars." The prince replied simply; "You too have changed." This suggests that he was watching me for a long time from the beyond…I ask him

"how did you know that your

artistic work would affect me so much?"

The prince, who himself is standing in etheric body a few centimetres from me, departs himself and turns his head down. He looks as if he was keeping a secret. It is up to me I have just enough time to say, "you are my angel" and he rises muttering "did you forget the secret code? that which will let you accomplish your mission on Earth? Search it!"

I have my latest vision of the prince of Idaho in early 2012. This was the most intense and the most emotional time of my existence until today. I see his face appear on the screen inside of my soul, an ethereal face, but alive.

He was not the same, his hair was shorter, he had this little shy smile and mischievous and affectionate gaze. Flabbergasted, I look first to his face looming on my mental screen and then plunge into his eyes as if the bottom of an ocean that I've known forever. The emotion I then feel is stronger than that which gave me my first love. I feel merged in that look, I feel alive like never-before in this world, within seconds I taste eternity. I understand that the love I was waiting for so long was not the first earthly love, but this eternal love between souls, the divine and pure love.

This quote from Paulo Coelho makes sense "The important meetings are planned by the souls long before the bodies meet" this is the meeting of two soulmates who are given appointments in time to reconnect. One died for guiding the other and

one was waiting for the other while

she was looking for everlasting love
in illusion and dreams.

Thirteen years between their birth dates
marked by the figure of the Trinity 3.
The Prince of Idaho died at 23 years
old, Laura narrowly escaped death and
saw her psychic gifts wake up at the
same age. She is the woman of whom
the Prince of Idaho had the vision, but
the connection does not end there,
both are linked by a divine mission
and the will to serve the Light
revealed through the outlet of
hallucinogens. From totally different
courses, the two souls seem to merge
into the same path. The mother of the
Prince of Idaho awoke soulless clones
that had been manipulated by society
at the age when her son died. The
parents of the prince have both had
visions after ingesting

sacred plants that revealed their source, their divine part, like Laura who had the revelation of her past life and vision of white light. The Prince of Idaho was aware of the divine light from his earliest childhood, raised in the Christic values, but also the humiliation and misery and never lost faith in the benevolence of the cosmos.

Laura woke up at 23 years old with a visit from her grandfather, but it is enlightenment and revelation of her previous life which fully made her conscious of the universal love and that's when she can write her book.
The Prince of Idaho, abused by a sect as a child, comes to the reincarnation of Tassem as a woman to show he has faith in her, an army of angels is at her side. Like him, she experienced rape, a dysfunctional family, addiction and social rejection. Like him, she awoke to love, to universal peace and shamanism. She did not seek God in churches but in

experiences at the border of our realities. There she realized that behind the fables and legends, hid authentic truth of any pre-existing dimension to life on Earth. She realized that in this previous life, she was just a man who had experienced the law of light. It's expressed through symbols, liturgy and rituals for understanding to the people who needed a more accessible truth. She was a 'Natural Mystic' as was the prince and his parents, an indigo child misunderstood in the world and isolated amid false believers and atheists. As Siddhartha Gautama sees the faces of humanity blend into the waves of the river in a single stream, the wave of the universal radiant fluid mixes our souls in the same way in the Universal Mind.

The Prince of Idaho came to reveal that he had faith in her and helped her through a secret code to pass the message of the source of love in the world, but the events wouldn't unfold in an obvious or easy way.

Following the coming of the Prince of Idaho, I feel the presence of evil spirits around me. I understand that by falling into whiskey and drugs, I will die without having accomplished my mission.

I wonder internally, "tell me my Prince of Idaho, what are the reasons for these visits? Are there any evil spirits ike the flipside of a coin to this kind of connection and this divine mission? After all, each light represents a dose of darkness. Even though I feel so much light every time I speak to you and when you appear to me my prince, I cannot help thinking that darkness is present around us too.

Is it normal to feel this fear?"

I barely formulated this thought to him that the phone starts ringing briskly. I remain paralyzed, leaving it to ring many times. I return to my senses and my strength and tell myself that I had a dream. I am finally able to pick up the handset and with a safe and strong voice I say "hello!" and then silence for a few seconds.

I hear a kind of music both fresh and disturbing, a kind of little sad church organ mixed with a gong from Tibetan bowls like those used in meditation, but I realize that the resonating percussion sounds feel disturbing and give me a chill running through my soul. I remain anchored to this bad feeling when I hear a male voice saying words in a dialect I do not know. This voice then seems to turn into something else with a kind of echo and a serious and deep tone. That's enough, it's almost

Indescribable, it reminds me of a sort of incantation. As soon as this person adopts a somewhat mechanical tone, a desire to invoke something and talking faster and insistently, I understand his bad intentions and I hang up the phone. I'm in panic,

but who in the afterlife would
want to hurt me?
Would this phone call that felt to be threatening a fatal blow, be an evil conspiracy from the beyond?
This is a fixed event such
as taking a photo.
I think of this event and this sentence of the Prince of Idaho that I had read in his memoirs.
"A photo can steal your soul."
It is why I make the link with these pictures of my grandmother and myself that I recovered a few years earlier and put in my personal collection. Our relationship had much degraded due to family tensions and I know from reliable source that she kept grudges

not to be reviewed at the end of her life when she was sick.

Fear drives me, I seize photos and burn them. On each of them burns my face first. Instinctively I seize my Indian jewelry that I kept for years in a box provided by my grandmother that also contained the prediction of the gypsy. At the time, I do not pay more attention to this detail. The bear paw that I place on my neck again awakens in me my warrior soul. I am ready to fight against these negative forces that have destroyed my life shattering predictions of my destiny, making my dog sick and preventing the success of my book. I want to find my amulet orca because when our totem animal is lost, our power is greatly weakened in the shamanic world. I'm searching the apartment, but I cannot find it. Gradually, I begin to realize that this deceased person, since her death was the cause of all my troubles because of her bad feeling towards me, she left with that sense of hatred and resentment that could lead to my exposure to the darkness.

The relationships within our family have been strained in the same time period. I think the whole family is possessed, an exorcist priest comes and confirms it to me. The exorcist confirmed that I must at all costs take off my bear paw necklace that was charged of my grandmother's energy by keeping it in her box. It is the same for the prediction of the gypsy that I must burn.

Before removing this bear paw one last fatal vision penetrates my mind: the image of my cousin as 'the heir'.
Knowing that my cousin was the favorite grandchild of my grandmother, I now understand that my death is desired by negative entities from the beyond. To consume all these bad vibrations, the last ritual is getting a symbol tattooed, representing the Prince of Idaho.

February 14th, 2012, I express the wish to include a letter on each finger of my right hand, but the tattoo artist refuses to tattoo every finger and insists that all the letters are tattooed on one finger. The name of the Prince of Idaho finds himself inscribed on my right ring finger. This tattoo looks suspiciously like an alliance, plus it is the right hand, where the widows wear their alliance. Then comes to my mind the vision the Prince of Idaho had of his future wife, the prediction of my grandfather and the alliance that chance has placed on my finger.

This lack of a ring is as the absence of our physical bodies, only our minds and writings bind us forever and are worth any form of physical expression that the world may live. This is a new form of bond that unites me to my Prince of Idaho. A metal ring cannot replace the magic of our mystical union. This tattoo translates the spiritual marriage of our souls in their purest and original energy. Your name on my skin is the burning seal of an ideal love, both born, yet not eternal. The thought of having this type of attachment and feelings that are akin to a loving relationship with that person who appears to me regularly, freezes my blood.

How is it possible to fall in love with someone who has been dead for many years? Must love always, be so cruel?

Necessarily doomed to fail because you've already gone to the other world, it defies all laws of time and space. I feel both linked forever to you, yet sad to not physically see you for our love was born and lives in the moment as the other couples in the world, but I think I'm lucky to live this unique and eternal happiness.

Then all has a price and if that is the price of eternity, I have no choice but to concede to this spiritual love that makes me feel every day, at once, both dead and alive. How long can this last? well, I do not know. I close my eyes and tell myself as long I am in this world, I will be separated from you, but you will always be with me to help me continue my path, our path? My road will be fraught with pitfall's. but I will remain strong for both of us my love.

But I realized with alarm that this tattoo, this shamanic ritual from beyond,
my only union with the Prince of Idaho, also enshrines the covenant of heaven and Earth in my prophetess persona.

Suddenly from this anchored tattoo on my skin, that represents the five letters of
the alliance starts shining a radiant light, I then think I have tamed the forces of

darkness by the power of the seal, but the curse will not stop during this episode.

Still in the grip of demonic spirits despite the intervention of the exorcist and my mother, pretending to worry about my sanity, put me in a psychiatric institute. I
now know that the evil trap has closed in on me when I see the look of demonic light coming from the psychiatrist. For years of confinement, I don't receive any more visits from the prince because of psych treatment inflicted on me that blur the contact between the two worlds.

After five years of hell and psychiatric medicated stupor, I wake up from my torpor at the Christ's age of 33.

Haunted for years by the memory of my visions of the Prince of Idaho, I have the feeling, a need to find a spark in my soul that makes me understand that I am not in error and that everything I experienced has a meaning. I am finally aware that the message of the Prince of Idaho is to write this book to tell our story.

.

I know the legend of the Prince of Idaho will serve as a gateway to market my first book. I change the title to the Phoenix of our Souls, I take the pseudonym Laura River as my artist name in memory of the prince and code the name and surname of the Prince of Idaho.

For all these years, I was aware of the code that was given to me, but countless judgments and mockery from unbelievers had made me give up, but since then the mystical code haunted me, in fact the name of the Prince of Idaho is a direct reference to the river of life that appears in the Bible, the Garden of Eden and the Apocalypse, but also in Native American prophecy of the Blue River. "And he showed me a river of life, clear as crystal, proceeding out of the throne of God and of the Lamb. In the middle of the town square and on both banks of the river there was a tree of life bearing twelve crops of fruit, yielding its fruit every month and whose leaves are for the healing of the nations."

The coming of the prince named after the river of life is the warning and the code of the coming of the revelation of the Word of the source of light on Earth.

It also carries the middle name of one of Tassem's brothers, Unktehi: the spirit of water and the symbol of the Phoenix, the constellation in which he was born, is the symbol of resurrection.

Relying on my mystical revelation with sacred plants I, Tassem am the prophetess, guardian of the soul and the Prince of Idaho is the river of life that will allow the revelation of the mystery of the universe in the Phoenix of our souls.

The only organization that exists to this day in honor of the new cult is the cosmic river connection. Veganism, planting sunflowers and wearing a pink bathrobe are common in this community.

Around the campfire, the Prince of Idaho whispers to the stars that he is missing his wife. Evil spirits retain her away from him in that other earthly world where medications weaken her mind and bring out her inner laziness. He cannot communicate with her since his beloved is retained in the chemical straitjacket. He knows that Laura is misplaced, lost and without a clue, unable to give meaning to her existence for many years now.

She does not want to live, just to join the other world where eternal love and her friends are waiting for her. A lifetime is too long before seeing her love.

But Laura has received this gift from God to write stories and before leaving she needs to tell their story and memories of the good old days, because yes happy days here appear dead, but are eternal in dream time. The small pink house in which she spent her holidays as a child now appears vanished into the clouds. She sees her little lady Neptune appear at the window of the house behind white curtains in a dream far away. It was the same route through Idaho that led to this little house.

The Prince of Idaho often watches Laura as she looks up to heaven and is lost in the constellation of the Phoenix, because that is where lies the land of the Prince of Idaho.

She knows that beyond this world alone, there is this light that shines forever and for her, this blinding white light, she contemplated it from the depths of her soul. a long time ago now.

She knows that the light will forgive her for shortening her life because she got to the awakening and has nothing more to discover or wait for on this Earth. She completed her earthly mission by writing the Phoenix of our souls, her unifying theory of the Light. It is through death that she will deliver the curse on her fate and the success of her first book and it is death that will lift the curse that prevents Laura and the Prince of Idaho living their love. She knows

that time does not exist in the realms of souls and that even if the years here below seem long, their cosmic connection is an eternal home.
He already imagines their reunion and their dreams in this big clearing.

Lady Neptune will jump around them while the prince plays James Taylor's Fire and Rain on his guitar. I know that I will see your face again ... stretched on the grass, near the giant sequoia and the tree house. They will speak of the Universal Mind and their trips with hallucinogenic mushrooms. Between old souls, they will take a look at the same cosmic rivers that had seen their birth.
Here, they're reunited on the other side of the mirror, contemplating the distant hallucination of earthly life. They vibrate in harmony, soulmates in a cascade of infinite light.
Laura is in the sky with diamonds and both have completed their divine mission.

They have incarnated, separated by time and space to better remember each other. In the clearing a wild horse neighing in the distance, the Prince of Idaho looks at it contemplatively, Laura knows this wild horse is a bit of the soul of the prince who is projected into space.

Then she closes her eyes for a moment after drinking a sip of Earl Gray and smoking a Winston. The Prince of Idaho is now dressed in a very New Age style and shows her a small bag of runes.

But the prince knows there is no future for them because they won't ever be embodied, then he throws the rune bag in the air with a chuckle.

The Prince of Idaho brings out a compass whose needle is constantly turning. He whispers, "why did you not follow earlier the path of your heart?" The compass needle stops directly in his direction.

Yes, Laura knew that in life everything is a sign and that the universe had conspired for their union, but evil spirits had been able to feed on the fear of Laura, by seizing her soul and pushing her family to hospitalize her. The neuroleptics have disrupted the brainwaves of Laura, she no longer had access to her visions and the discourse of psychiatrists had sown disorder and confusion in her mind.

Yet still lived the memory of her prince in her mind and her heart knew it was not lying.

Regardless of all, this is nothing but a dark memory that Laura is now released from forever.

Both are pure souls who sacrificed time in their earthly life, both were indigo children who came from the stars, very aware of the universal interconnection between human being, nature and animals.

It was strongly inscribed in their DNA. They wanted to work to heal the planet authentically as such pure and generous souls, conscious of others and keeping the hope that humanity raises its vibrations.

They were not only children of Gaia, they were children of the cosmos, conscious of dancing spirals of galaxies around them, the vibrations of the earth and volcanoes, lava quivering in their soul.

But despite their spirituality, both were too fragile for this world and not meant to live long, they both drowned in alcohol and drugs. The prince tragically died in mysterious circumstances.

The prince was probably pushed to death by the Kingdom of Shadows, (he dreamed that the spirits were taking his life), who did not want a missionary of God fulfilling his potential. The jealousy of a little sparrow and gypsies killed him, but it was a blessing in disguise because from another dimension he could do what he could not do on Earth, contact Laura.

Laura in turn was not far from death when her family made it to the hospital. Many years after, death called to Laura. Laura burnt her wings and was caught in the trap of psychiatry that killed her soul.

An Indian proverb says that what is tragic in death is not so much the death but what dies in you during your lifetime.

And that's the dark experience that happened to Laura, but she knows that in the afterlife her soul will be returned to her, healed from the reach of earthly life.

Both are star crossed lovers who

have experienced a sad fate.

But she knew that their divine mission would end in their resurrection in the higher dimensions and thus the Last Crusade would be fulfilled. The Prince of

Idaho sacrificed to wait for Laura on the other side and inspire in her their legend.
And once their legend is written,

Laura just needs to join him.

"Where your treasure is, your heart will be also. God cannot be mocked." The Prince of Idaho sings one of his favorite songs "maybe God's a woman too."

He knows that on his return Tassem is reincarnated as a woman, and this woman is Laura River, his wife. No, she didn't go to the town hall to marry a dead man, but in memories of these visions, she carries as an alliance, the tattooed ring on her finger of her right hand.

Widowed, each in their kingdom, their

love cursed by the number 13 marking the thirteen years that separated their respective births, lovers of the cosmos united by the vision, are beyond this life together forever. The two shamans wait and feel each other shuddering at the touch of another kingdom. The army of Kachina dolls stand guard at their side until the time of the Apocalypse.

Only Laura and her allied spirits know the imminence of divine revelation. She knows the dark plot against her and the servants of Light.

Laura retains poetic writings like prisoners at the bottom of a dusty drawer, hoping they are known one day, the mystical writings of the Phoenix of our souls and the legend of the Prince of Idaho.
These books are like messages in a bottle thrown into the sea which she hopes that one day or another will touch the hearts of people.

The constellation of the Phoenix under which they are both born protects their love. The Phoenix is the symbol of their mystical union and the immortality of their relationship in the afterlife.

It is also the first Christian symbol of the resurrection of Christ. In a truly shamanic process, and a sort of divine grace, water and fire washed Laura's injuries and purified her soul.

The Prince of Idaho, the spirit of the river, completed his prophecy and if the Devil defeated Laura of her earthly time, she knows the promise of the firebird and the balance will be restored from the other realm.

It seems to me I always notice the scent of the distant fragrant sands of the Arizona desert when he comes to me. I cannot put into words this so subtle and indefinable smell.

Finally, he appears to me beyond the veil of death, he stands before me in the same white and radiant halo that illuminates the outline of his spiritual body that my deathly body cannot embrace. Where his body begins, where ends this mysterious light ...

My lover of the cosmos finally comes for me for our last trip. This is more of a game of stealth, but all for our eternal union. When he becomes almost tangible, he lays his delicate fingers on my freshly inked tattoo, there is still the mark of redness around it that becomes radiant on contact, he begins to smile shyly. We stay there, watching intently, his eyes light up more and more, now I know that eternity is offered to me,

to contemplate the glow of his eyes
where my universe begins and ends.

Then it seems to me that the wind of
the distant desert intensifies. I wear
an Indian traditional dress of purple in
a style that is both refined and
noble… my wedding dress! beyond
this dress, I see my last majestic totem
animal, the phoenix shines from my
subtle body at the time of my visit in
the hereafter. This bird of flaming
fire, my divine symbol of
resurrection. The smell of the desert
has come back to me, it fills the
atmosphere completely. I remember
now of its meaning; formerly young
Indian lovers painted their faces of
each other with the desert sand to
express their commitment to the Great
Spirit. Only discrete and sensitive
beings who did not dare declare their
love, were performing this ritual. To
my amazement, he redoubled his
smile without showing his teeth, his
lips form a beautiful curve,

very harmonious and full of goodwill,
he nods:
"you, my twin soul, I come for you
to form that one eternal Phoenix that
will blend with the constellation that
bears the same devoted name and
will continue to sparkle in the
coming millennia of its incandescent
glow."

We both smile, unable to touch with our physical bodies, of which we have no more, but we burn a common energy, the energy of our souls already merged.

The desert wind fills the space and invites us to recreate this atmosphere of indescribable physical promiscuity. Our two souls of shamans are meeting in this intoxicating breath through this feeling of love and compassion in the highest degree and most infinite. This is the first fragrance of paradise that comes to me and now that I have joined my prince, we already fly away beyond fertile landscapes across fields radiating love.

The sacred phoenix grants admission with a flapping wing, to all the wandering souls, recalcitrant to light, releasing the shade and bringing them the peace of the divine and in the flight of our subtle body we forget that we're no longer flesh or blood and he gives me a tender kiss, that promises our heavenly union.

My Prince of Idaho listen out for me in a seashell and call for me once more where can go off together in our Volkswagen bus. We will take the roads just for the pleasure of taking them because every road leads somewhere. Sometimes we stop at the seaside to hear the murmur of water and wind crying the agony of Mother Earth and even in the rain forest, we will hug trees bruised by human destruction. We will be infinite and free, cleansed of all suffering and of any penalty provided by terrestrial life. My soul is so light with fluid and subtle waves, like we could travel forever in the endless universe that creates our thinking. You'll fill your lungs with helium, and you'll tell me what you told me when we met, "I'd like to have a deep relationship with a beautiful woman… in love at first sight".

You'll show me the portraits you did of me before meeting me and I'll do the same.

We will dance in the clearing,
playing, holding our hands into the
air, you'll tell me, "you see it is I who
saw you first, I was for a long time
watching you in the clouds and I was
waiting for you to see me. You gave
me a bit of your skin by tattooing my
name on you and that of our country
as Lady Neptune's. We will be in this
ritual, forever

as the three bees."

"Do you know that it is the anniversary of our wedding? today is February 14th" whispers the Prince of Idaho and on the cake is written "Play it again Sam" which makes the prince and I smile tenderly. We have many secret codes between us, and it amuses me.

By the time we blow out the candles, a UFO passes over our heads. The Prince of Idaho is not surprised and sighs, "I remember, like it was cool when they took me in the flying saucer."
"Thank you, Holy Mother of UFOS" it doesn't surprise by me either, after all, you deserved this trip as much as any another in the billions of stars, planets, galaxies and universes. "So, we will have a fucking beer and eat pizza that you have prepared for us" that reminds me of the good old days with Lady Neptune and you'll tell me you love me to death.

"Many people, if you were still on Earth, would find you weird talking about flying saucers" I say, chuckling.
"We're all a little weird, after all" he answers with a sigh and then "I'm not weird, I 'm cosmic!"
"And you, weren't you weird when you had such cool trips with Hawaiian mushrooms?!"

"I was already almost in Idaho actually" I retorted, smiling. "Yes, complete with a pink robe" he replied.
"And Lady Neptune, your cosmic friend

licking your empty beer cans wearing her doggy diaper." Jim Morrison will mingle at the party beckoning me to come and talk. I remember those days! "Do not forget that I am your psychedelic teacher" Jim whispered "remember when I dictated poems to you and that you went to see me at Père Lachaise cemetery in Paris with your friend FloFlo? Damn it, that was cool. I also remember the good times you spent in the city of Angers with your friend Bryan. Ah the good old days."

And Kurt Cobain will arrive reciting "it's better to burn out than to fade away… Whatever, never mind ..." All four of us will play a game of poker and the Prince of Idaho will whisper in my ear: "You remember the card I laid at the foot of your bed?" "Yes, of course!" I reply. "Well, it was me! It was to tell you that your trip to Idaho would run well and you know I'm a joker. You see I have kept my pinkie swear!" There will also be my grandfather, he'll

come unexpectedly, put his hands
over my eyes and asks me
"who is it?" as he did when I was a
child. There will be a party full of
people, I'll repent of my sins and I will
forgive those who have offended me,
it will be all peace and love.

I know your preferred dimension is
the Pink dimension and your
psychedelic soul surfs its waves,
but we care about Gaia and its
evolution so, we will continue
to work among the light guides to

prepare the ascent of Earth.

Finally, the time comes for the
Apocalypse, revelation and the
kingdom from below will receive the
message of love of Tassem, the
guardian of the soul.

And you my prince of Idaho will mix
your legend with that of Tassem, your
soul connected with the release of its
cycle of incarnations.

special thanks to joanne Hersom for the translation from French to English.

Edition : Books on Demand,
12/14 rond-Point des Champs-Elysées, 75008 Paris
Impression : BoD - Books on Demand, Norderstedt, Allemagne
ISBN : 9782322190959
Dépôt légal : Décembre 2019